Cinderella

QED
QED Publishing

Once upon a time, there lived an unhappy young girl. Her mother had died and her father had married a widow with two daughters.

Her stepmother doted on her own daughters.
Nothing was too good for them –
dresses, shoes, parties...
whatever they wanted.

But, for the poor unhappy girl,
there was nothing at all.

Her dresses were her
stepsisters' hand-me-downs.

Her dinner was nothing but scraps.

Her day was filled with hard work.

Only when evening came was she allowed to
sit for a while by the fire, near the cinders.
Everybody called her Cinderella.

One day, beautiful new dresses arrived at the
house. A ball was to be held at the palace and
the stepsisters were invited.

Cinderella didn't ask if she could go, too.
She knew very well what the answer would be.

Instead, Cinderella began her chores.
She washed the dishes, scrubbed the floors
and turned down the beds.

"I am so unhappy," she sighed.

Suddenly, as Cinderella was all alone, a fairy appeared.

"Don't be alarmed, Cinderella," said the fairy.
"I am your Fairy Godmother. I know you'd love to go to the ball. And so you shall!"

"But I'm dressed in rags," sighed Cinderella.

The Fairy Godmother smiled.
With a flick of her magic wand,
Cinderella found herself wearing
the most beautiful dress she had
ever seen.

Cinderella was speechless.

"Now for your coach," said the Fairy Godmother. "Bring me a pumpkin!"

Then the Fairy Godmother turned to the cat. "Bring me seven mice."

Cinderella soon returned with the pumpkin, and the cat with seven mice.

With a flick of her magic wand, the Fairy Godmother turned the pumpkin into a sparkling coach. Next, she turned the mice into six white horses and a coachman.

Cinderella could hardly believe her eyes.

"There is one condition," said the Fairy Godmother. "The magic will wear off on the last stroke of midnight, so you must be home by then."

"I will. Thank you, Fairy Godmother," beamed Cinderella.

Cinderella had a wonderful time at the ball,
dancing with the prince himself.

Then when she heard the first stroke of midnight, without a word of goodbye, she slipped from the prince's arms and ran down the steps.

As she ran, she lost one of her slippers. Still,
away she fled and vanished into the night.

The prince was now madly in love with her.

He picked up the slipper and said to his
ministers, "Search everywhere for the girl
whose foot this slipper fits. I will never be
happy until I find her!"

The ministers tried the slipper on the foot of every girl in the land, until only Cinderella was left.

"That awful, untidy girl simply cannot have been at the ball," snapped her stepmother. "The prince ought to marry one of my two daughters! Can't you see how ugly Cinderella is?"

To everyone's amazement, the shoe fitted perfectly.

The Fairy Godmother appeared and waved her magic wand. In a flash, Cinderella was transformed.

In an elegant dress, Cinderella shone with youth and beauty. Her stepmother and stepsisters gaped at her in amazement.

The ministers had found the prince's love.
Cinderella and the prince married the very
next day and lived happily ever after.

Notes for parents and teachers

- Look at the front cover of the book together. Can the children guess what the story might be about? Read the title together. Does this give them more of a clue?

- When the children first read the story or you read it together, can they guess what might happen in the end?

- What do the children think of the characters? Is the stepmother kind? What about the Fairy Godmother? Who is their favourite character and why?

- The villain in this story is the stepmother. Can the children think of any other stories with a similar character?

- When Cinderella goes to the ball, do the children think she will be discovered? Are the children glad that Cinderella marries the prince?

- What would the children do if they had a fairy godmother and could make one wish? Ask the children to draw or paint their own fairy godmother.

- What other endings can the children think of? Perhaps the children can act out the story, and then the new endings.

- Cinderella is hard-working and is rewarded by the Fairy Godmother. Ask the children what jobs they could do at home and what rewards they could receive.

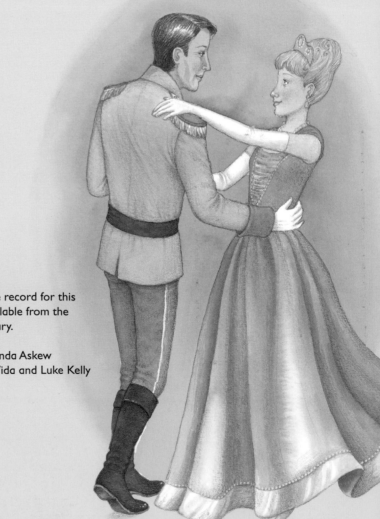

Copyright © QED Publishing 2010

First published in the UK in 2010 by QED Publishing
A Quarto Group Company
226 City Road
London EC1V 2TT

www.qed-publishing.co.uk

ISBN 978 1 84835 485 2

Printed in China

A catalogue record for this book is available from the British Library.

Editor: Amanda Askew
Designers: Vida and Luke Kelly